Lightness

Lightness

a novel

FANIE DEMEULE

translated by ANITA ANAND

First published in French by Hamac, Montreal.
Copyright © Hamac. Published by permission of Hamac.
Original title, *Déterrer les os*.
Copyright © Anita Anand, 2020, for the translation.

All rights reserved. No part of this book may be reproduced, for any reason or by any means, without permission in writing from the publisher.

The following is a work of fiction. Many of the locations are real, although not necessarily as portrayed, but all characters and events are fictional and any resemblance to actual events or people, living or dead, is purely coincidental.

Copyediting: Kaiya Cade Smith Blackburn
Author photo: Émilie Lamothe
Cover design: Debbie Geltner
Book design: Tika eBooks

Library and Archives Canada Cataloguing in Publication

Title: Lightness : a novel / Fanie Demeule ; translated by Anita Anand.
Other titles: Déterrer les os. English
Names: Demeule, Fanie, 1990- author. | Anand, Anita, 1962- translator.
Description: Translation of: Déterrer les os.
Identifiers: Canadiana (print) 20190219653 | Canadiana (ebook) 20190220287 | ISBN 9781773900520 (softcover) | ISBN 9781773900537 (HTML) | ISBN 9781773900544 (Kindle) | ISBN 9781773900551 (PDF)
Classification: LCC PS8607.E4877 D4813 2019 | DDC C843/.92—dc23

Printed and bound in Canada.
The publisher gratefully acknowledges the support of the Government of Canada through the Canada Council for the Arts, the Canada Book Fund, and of the Government of Quebec through the Société de développement des entreprises culturelles (SODEC).

We acknowledge the financial support of the Government of Canada through the National Translation Program for Book Publishing, an initiative of the Action Plan for Official Languages – 2018-2023: Investing in Our Future, for our translation activities.

Linda Leith Publishing
Montreal
www.lindaleith.com

For Gabriel

Again she raises her hand to her breast, to the dying flower whose scent slips beyond the garden and drifts to the sea.

"Perhaps it's that flower," someone suggests, "the scent is so strong."

"No, I'm used to it. It's nothing really."

— Marguerite Duras, *Moderato Cantabile*, translated by Richard Seaver

I've already told you that I came into this world a little early.

I weigh four pounds. I brown in the incubator for a good while, intubated like a little chicken that needs to be fattened up in a hurry.

Once out of the hospital, I don't remain a runt for very long. I never stop suckling; I'm bottomless. Within a month, I make up the missing pounds, to the detriment of the mental and physical health of my mother, who soon relegates me to bottles of Similac. I'm a baby on vacuum mode.

In the last world, my hunger must have been so great that it could never be appeased in this life.

.

I'm at the seaside. My mother and father, on either side of me, hold my hands. We're waiting in line. I have ice cream sundae all over my face. Its overpowering taste completely satisfies me. All around us, the blinking colours of the rides flash in a delirious frenzy. I get a giant buzz: so much beauty to be taken in at once. I'm one and a half.

The line comes to an end. The wooden carousel appears. The most extraordinary thing I will see in my whole life. The horses' movements frozen in mid-race, the pigs' and roosters' too. A majestic circle festooned with the golden light of bulbs as big as my head. I am placed on a yellow pony.

The ride starts to shake. Magical music emanates from its heart, rises into the night. I'm hallucinating. We go around, then once more, and once more again. I pass my parents every time, and they smile and wave at me. And it begins anew. I discover perfection. I want it to go on forever.

The carousel slows down and stops. The music ends, with brutal suddenness. My mother smiles at me. It's over.

My father tries to get me off the pony. In vain. He finally allows me a second ride.

Transported by the music, I immediately find my way back to a state of bliss, even more intense now than the first time. The smiling, the photos, the waving hands.

To my great disappointment, the moment ends, again. I am consumed with despair.

My parents let me go on a third time, then a fourth, and then once more, and once more after that. The fair is about to close. We have to leave. My face is hot, insane with pain and pleasure.

My father scoops up his little addict. My mother tries to calm me down. Impossible to manage grief of this magnitude. I watch the carousel fade away in the ocean of sparkling lights. I cry.

Somewhere in my brain, one zone turns off, and another lights up. I understand that everything has to end, and that this is just the way things are in the natural scheme of things. I was born and I died on a wooden pony.

.

My mother goes away and leaves me in my godmother's capable hands. What my godmother doesn't know is that my world revolves around excess. Whenever it's time to wean me, I throw a tantrum.

My mother had let her know that I love grapefruit. So, she arrives with a whole case.

At snack time, she brings me to the table and slices a nice, juicy, pink one. The aroma of paradise splashes my face and wakes up the monster in me. I begin to choke on my saliva.

She brings the first piece to my mouth, and the momentum is unleashed. The pulp of this grapefruit is so perfectly and deliciously sweet that I need more, many more, so I can have this taste on my tongue forever.

I eat a grapefruit, then, from somewhere deep and guttural inside me, demand another. More, I order her. My godmother cuts up another grapefruit and I immediately devour it. Grunting, I ask for more. I suck up the juice until the fruit is nothing more than an empty, dry piece of rind.

After the sixth one, she calls my mother.

"Your daughter's eaten a lot of grapefruit. She's already had six and she wants another one. Should I give it to her?"

"No. She could go on forever."

She's right.

Whenever I'm told that something has to stop, a part of me breaks down a little more.

·

During the first years of my life, whenever I arrive at my grandfather's house, he laughs and sings a song that goes, "As long as there's something in the fridge." My grandparents receive the briefest greeting from me, a greeting to satisfy the minimal requirements of politeness, before I dash straight to the fridge, or the candy cupboard, or the box of Danish shortbread. I seize everything within reach, even the black licorice, which I hate.

I'm not sure my grandmother finds that funny.

My mother decrees that I must not be laughed at, as if I were handicapped. I don't care. What's important is what's in my mouth.

I wonder what is so special about my behaviour.

·

My grandfather reads to me. He tells me disquieting tales: of ghosts, of a mechanical nightingale, and of an endless winter. Tales spangled with the sublime, and with dread. He sings me songs, not just the one about the refrigerator. My grandfather sings, and the blue jays caw in the cedar trees near the lake. We walk around the big meadow in the shade of Mount Orford.

I stuff myself with his stories, his words; I drown in them. They become as real as everything else. My mind begins to fill with their spectres.

Walking in the woods surrounding the cottage, I feel the trees' shadow on my skin. The old trunks squeak, and life swarms around me. Sometimes, deep in the woods, there's a broken shell lying on the ground, and you can see a poor little chick inside, all curled-up and shriveled. In the fields at the end of the road, flowers blaze in the sunshine and crushed grass snakes cook on the dirt roads.

The water from the spring flows between my fingers, amazingly cold and silky. Muddy pebbles give way beneath my feet. I dislike looking at the seaweed at the bottom of lakes and streams. The sight of these long, stretching arms claws at my stomach. I imagine myself buried under the mud at their roots, wrapped in their cool clamminess. I also hate seeing rocks emerging from the depths. Their black silhouette, sinisterly passive, unsettles me.

I avoid looking below the water's surface.

The swirling water grows dark, the forest quiet, and I return to the cottage. I open the fridge and stuff myself, filling the little holes that are growing inside me.

My grandfather sits in his armchair and gradually begins to die from the inside. He laughs less and less, doesn't sing anymore. A slow, abrasive death, born somewhere in his kidneys. He doesn't know it yet.

My mother's scared. Of strangers, accidents, robberies, crazy people, and dogs. When I go out walking by myself I can't go past the bicycle path, which is three houses from ours. I'm not allowed to cross Chambly Road. The further you venture, the greater the risk. From the other side of the street, everything seems dangerous to me.

I never dare transgress these boundaries.

I'm recruited in swimming class. The teacher tells my parents that I have good endurance and that he sees me on his racing team. Endurance that comes from no one knows where. I accept, for no reason at all.

I have no competitive spirit. I don't care about winning or losing. The truth is that I absolutely loathe everything about swimming: the chemical smell that greets me as I enter the sports complex, the rubber swimming caps I'm forced to wear and which cause my hair to break, the inevitable shock of the cold water when I jump in, the total discomfort of the whole experience, which does not leave me, even long after getting out of the pool, the showers, the changing rooms and the sports complex with its slippery floor.

Despite everything, I go. I take part in the competitions though I feel completely indifferent about them. While my arms beat the water around my head, and my legs flap along behind me, my mind stays focused on the pizza that awaits me. I can smell it, taste it already. I hear the crunch of its fine crust. It's the pizza that guides me, that gives me the strength to keep going. The after-swimming pizza that makes up for the horrible experience of this chlorinated bath.

My father says that it tastes like cardboard and that it's too expensive. For me, it is perfection itself. My edible medal, my promised, deserved reward.

After some time, I decide that I can't take it anymore. In the sports centre parking lot, before a practice, I tell my father that my stomach hurts too much. He looks at me and says, "You want to stop for good, don't you?" Yup, that's pretty much it. He isn't angry. Maybe just a little disappointed.

We go directly to Pizza Hut, and then home.

I never go back to the pool again. Pizza, on the other hand, comes back, week after week, into my mouth.

.

At recess, I snack on ramen. A guy in grade six tells me I should watch what I eat. It's supposed to be a piece of advice.

It's not to be mean. It's for my good. I'm fat. The sentence doesn't go away.

Some people say that I am "built," or "chubby," or "big-boned." My grandmother prefers to say I look "solid." I wonder: are other people liquid?

The year I turn eight, the ice storm catches hold of winter and of my grandfather's death. The first person close to me to die. The only thing I remember from his funeral is the surreal coolness of his cheek, the overwhelming smell of incense, and the sound of my sister bawling in church, terrorized by the bellowing sound coming down from the organ.

I didn't want to attend the burial.

It takes me a while to realize the impact of his disappearance. I don't understand until some months later when we go lay flowers on his grave. My sister asks my mother if Grandpa has become a skeleton. My mother breaks down, completely, all at once, just dissolves into tears.

I imagined his bones. They stayed, embedded like that, in my head.

The summer I turn eight I become claustrophobic.

I wake up one morning in the soiled bed and I believe this is the end. I had never heard of menstruation. My mother hears me screaming and she comes running. Defeated, she repeats, "No, not already. No."

She explains the business about babies to me. Has me come downstairs to the bathroom. Opens the medicine cabinet and shows me a sanitary napkin. I remember having found some in a bag under the sink. I'd thought they were enormous bandages, and had a great time decorating the sides of the bath with them. Never had I imagined having to stuff them in my underwear someday.

My mother shows me what to do with them, and how to dispose of them afterwards. Like for a diaper, you have to change it. I'm mortified. I cannot believe that I will have to do this for the rest of my life. If this is what it means to become a woman, I don't want it.

All day I weep in anger and helplessness, against this excessive body, this cunning, vicious body that I begin to loathe and dread. This humiliating stranger. This diving bell in which I'm trapped, buried alive.

·

The first day of my period, we go and visit my godmother at her cottage. It's hot. Everyone goes swimming except me. I stay hidden in the shadows, sweating in the basement, where the ceilings are covered in long-legged spiders. I stay here and wait for the flow to stop.

·

Sitting cross-legged in my Babysitting course, I feel it gushing between my legs. Dampness on my bum.

I stand up and see a glossy stain stamped on the gymnasium floor. I ask the instructor permission to run to the bathroom. She refuses, reminds me that we're doing a test. I go back and sit on my scarlet puddle, hoping to hide it. I look around me. Nobody seems to have noticed this anomaly. Nobody knows that I have my period, not even my best friends, my brother or my sister. Only my parents know.

I dread the moment when I will have to get up. My thoughts race about, trying to come up with strategies to hide the stain on my pants when I walk to my locker, where I will finally be able to tie my coat around my waist.

In the bathtub, at home, I tell myself that this is a nightmare. I'm crying, gasping. The water is red and full of globs that smell metallic. My mother returns from work. She walks up the stairs and hears me moaning. She comes in and leans over the bathtub ledge. Taking care not to touch the water, she kisses me and wraps her arms around my shoulders. I tell her everything.

The Babysitting course instructor fails me. I won't get my babysitting licence.

My mother calls her to find out why. I'm not mature enough. I'd tried to sneak away during an important evaluation.

At the La Ronde ticket counter, I feel my flow begin. Without a word to my friends, I tear off to the bathroom. I empty out my backpack. No Kotex. And no more toilet paper. I'm too embarrassed to ask the person in the next stall. The minutes tick by; I hear my friends calling me. I open the little metal garbage can by the toilet bowl. Under a couple of tissues, I find a Maxi pad that isn't too bad, and try to make it stick to my already smeared panties.

I pull up my pants, shivering with horror.

That day, I ride the Monster three times without realizing it. All I feel is the prolonged contact of my skin against the blood of an unknown person.

There must be some way to stop having periods. Sooner or later, I'll figure it out. From now on, this is my one goal in life.

I begin by asking my parents at suppertime. They're a bit bewildered by my question. They tell me that athletes, gymnasts and ballerinas sometimes stop menstruating. But that it takes a long time, and is pretty rare.

They explain to me that a body has its limits. When it puts too much energy in certain areas, there isn't any more left for other things, like periods.

Now I've got to transfer my energy into something. I try sit-ups. Easier said than done.

When I turn on the television, the sight of Olympic sprinters or contortionists from the Cirque du Soleil fills me with both hate and admiration. Dressed in tight costumes, they all have the same body: flat stomach, arms that are slender and firm, no hips, no breasts. Like boys. In my head, these are the disencumbered, and they are perfect.

After elementary school, I start attending a private high school, while my friends go to a public one. The beginning of a long period of solitude. I start biting my nails until they bleed.

I read Victor Hugo and *The Lord of the Rings* at lunchtime, in the school library, and other thick books that look serious. I'm a nerd.

In the world of The Sims, I'm popular, I organize parties and I'm skinny.

In real life, I'm fat and I don't have a lot of friends.

I decide I want to play the cello.

Everything happens quickly. I register for lessons; my parents buy me the instrument.

My teacher notes the power of my sound. My bow and my fingers press themselves deeply into the strings. My heaviness resonates through my cello; the weight of me sings.

My school uniform pinches everywhere. The buttons are all about to pop. I choose the longer kind of skirt to hide my thigh gelatin. I'm not obese but I'm generously chubby. There's surely lots to fix. My fat cheeks, flabby breasts, arms that sag like those of old women, I don't even know where to start. This body is just too much, everywhere. It displays its excessive pleasure, swollen by repeated, daily abuses. A mass that gradually grew into itself thanks to perpetual indulgences. Even the expression in my eyes seems placid, dull, as if satiated.

There's this friend at school who weighs exactly the same as me. I know, because we weigh ourselves, one after the other, and the needle goes up to the same critical number.

My friend couldn't care less. Unlike me. Her indifference disgusts me as much as our weight.

We eat a bag of Cheetos in her basement. It smells like orange, modified milk substance cheese. I start feeling too hot. Sitting on the floor, I examine our thighs pressed against each other, similarly badly shaved, white and flabby. A new, uncomfortable feeling settles inside me. I suddenly know that this feeling is there to stay. I'm overwhelmed by a kind of nausea that forces me to push the bag far away from me, and to cover my thighs.

A visceral sort of shame.

I tell my friend I am going to the bathroom and dash into her room instead to call my father. When he arrives, my friend asks me why I don't want to sleep over anymore. I tell her that I feel like throwing up.

Once I get home, I put on my black bathing suit and climb the ladder of the above-ground pool. Ten o'clock, a night in June that stinks of skunk and fresh chlorine. I contemplate my deformed reflection for a moment on the smooth surface of the water. I jump in. The freezing water slices my skin with its sharp, moving blades.

I'm out of breath after one lap around the pool. But I keep going. Without stopping, I obstinately flap my arms and legs, contract my muscles. No stopping, no letting go of the tension. I read that in "Your Best Body Ever for Back to School" in the last issue of *Seventeen* magazine. When I'm about to begin my seventh lap, I think I could continue going on this ride forever. Until everything is burned off, and everything starts over from the beginning. My body like a brand new, empty file.

Two months later, the scales display a loss of thirty-five pounds. I pursue my nocturnal laps around the pool.

In the class picture at the start of the new school year I have smaller cheeks than on the one from the year before. I'm proud of myself. I'm on the right track.

At the break, I hurry to the back of the schoolyard where I hide with my lunch. One Quaker granola bar which I savour, one tiny bite at a time. I study to make the most of my hour-long break. I want my marks to be record-smashing. High school is ending, and I want to finish with a bang.

I wear the short skirt which reveals my toned legs. Unbutton the top of my shirt to expose my beautiful new collarbones.

In the hallways, I begin greeting people and receive many smiles in return, especially from boys. For the first time, I am visible to the world. I begin to believe that I can become someone.

·   ·

A too-heavy door swings shut on my back one day as I'm carrying my cello. The wood splits with a loud crack, unequivocally. A write-off. My parents buy me another one.

·

I get better.

At night I practise over and over, lulled by the steady noise of the metronome. Its flat resonance bores into the walls of my brain where it dislodges all traces of inaccuracy and of excess.

One morning, while coming down the stairs that lead to the lockers, I lose consciousness and tumble down the flight of steps. I open my eyes as someone is lifting my feet. I haven't hurt myself. I discover how good it is to faint, to fall, to feel yourself just go away. I spend the rest of the day in the nurse's office, glowing.

Afterwards, I keep doing it; I faint from time to time.

My mother, increasingly worried, finally brings me to the clinic. I'm probed, all over. My doctor calls what happens to me blood pressure drops and says they are neither serious nor dangerous. Benign is the word he uses.

It's time for me to register for Cégep. I ask my sister to hide two words behind her back. In one hand is the word "literature;" in the other, "fine arts." I choose the left one.

During my poetry presentation our eyes meet. He has pale skin and long, dark hair. Not really my type, but he seems sweet. He raises his hand and says that he likes my style. Something about the way he says that makes him sound like a suck-up.

He waits for me after class, asks me if I want to go to a play, the same evening. Curious, I accept.

My first date.

The play is so bad that it's embarrassing. We chat. We go to a bar. He isn't old enough either, but he has a moustache. He orders two beers and some nachos appear on the table. I don't move.

"You're not having any?"

"No. I'm not hungry. And also, I'm too fat."

This confession is blurted out, just like that; I have no idea why. I'm immediately mad at myself. He turns around and looks at me, his head cocked.

"I don't know where you got that idea. Honestly!"

I nevertheless notice that he doesn't say the opposite. He must find me fat as well.

With an air of nonchalance, I take a chip, followed by another. I empty the basket without even realizing it. And then I'm in a bad mood, and I start to find our conversation tedious. I'm wasting my time. I abruptly ask my date to take me home. He gets up without a protest, but I see that he senses something about me, a kind of dull pain.

On the front step he kisses me and invites me to supper the next day, at his father's house. I just want to get out of it, but I say yes.

I run into my room, change and jump into the swimming pool, which receives me tenderly in its icy arms.

.

After supper, between the trees at the back of his garden, his tongue pokes around in my mouth.

His father eats by himself in the house. Slumped in front of a blank TV screen, eating cold ravioli out of a tin with a spoon.

My date talks to me about his feelings. I don't listen. I only understand his tongue in my mouth and his hands, his uncountable fingers that rock me where I've never been rocked before. His hands, which talk to me about things that I like to feel, under the sick tree in the garden. The bark comes off in strips on my skin, while the mouldy apples fall. He talks about things that are absent — like me: I look at him from far away, through the darkness.

His head is encircled by Chinese shadows, and his eyes have green rings. It's his father's insomnia that lances his skin, and his ghost that haunts his gaze.

He tells me he wants me to stay the night. I like his hands on my body, his hands which make me continue to play with his heart, a heart which is already getting ready to be broken.

A shadow freezes at the window; his father is watching us. I can see the can of Chef Boyardee in his hand. He has the inertia of a corpse.

His son wants me to belong to him. He slips me an "I love you" at the outer rim of my ear. I get up quickly, fall on the apples that burst under my hands, get up again to flee. He grabs my arm.

"You're leaving?"

"No, I just have to go to the bathroom."

I enter the house, which smells of ravioli and cold cigarettes. His father is watching me from his armchair like a king who has been dead for centuries. He is listening to the Beatles and smiling at me. Uncomfortable, I forget to acknowledge him. Instead, I leave without a sound and walk from Chambly to Longueuil. The streetlamps guide me all the way home, where I get in bed, completely shattered.

Two days and two nights go by. I finally call him back, I forge ahead, with no courage. I have to tell him. That I don't love him.

"Listen. I have something to tell you. This isn't easy."

His broken voice answers me, as dry as the tree in his garden.

"Me too. I've got something to tell you. My father died. Yesterday."

·

I don't know what happens to him after that. He doesn't come to class anymore; he stops coming to Cégep altogether. I only think about one thing, the worst, his body lying under the apple tree, next to his dad's.

Years later, he sits right across the métro from me, by chance. I stick my head in my book so that he won't notice me. I feel his gaze settling on the gnawed tips of my fingers.

·

It's the summer I turn seventeen. I go to the Magdalen Islands with my family, to our ancestral home, for four weeks. A month as a challenge, an ultimatum. A month to melt and unearth my bones.

There are endless footpaths on the island. I spend the lull before supper roaming the forest and forgetting my hungry stomach. My body firms up quite a bit. I only eat the most frugal of meals. Half an orange, a small mound of pasta, a ladle full of soup. I'd rather hear my empty stomach gurgling like a water gourd, so I can fill it with the smells of kelp and pebbles. Feel that my body, lying spread out under the rising tide, holds together by the thinnest of threads, ready to dissolve into foam, into spray, atop the crest of the waves.

When it rains, I walk outside into the August storm. The sky roars. Thrilled, I lie down on the narrow waterline that divides the ocean from its shore and imagine my body dissipating in this violent natural environment, sublimated by the powerful sea squalls. The freezing water penetrates me, and I shiver with pleasure.

I know that something big is about to happen. I hear the mermaids calling me from the depths of their ocean trenches.

At the end of August, I meet you. You have a blue gaze, ruddy skin. Your huge smile. I don't ask myself any more questions. I know that you're the one I need and no one else, and I see in your eyes that you think the same thing about me.

We're at a party. The evening has just begun and you offer me a glass of gin, or maybe something even stronger. The only thing I remember is that a second later we are in a bed upstairs and I'm lying in your arms. Our shoes thrown over the blankets. I bring my hands to your face to be sure that you are there, and my fingers explore your mouth. I can feel what you are saying through the tips of my fingers. You're saying, "I could die."

Suddenly my head feels as if it's coming unscrewed; I urgently need to go to the bathroom. On the way, someone I don't know lands on top of me, and then everything starts falling. In a fraction of a second my head falls off, bursts as it lands. We're outside, I remember the cold. I have no idea what is happening but I do know that this guy is on top of me and that I do nothing to get out from under him, that had I been a corpse nothing would have been any different.

Once he's done he gets up; he takes off.

A silhouette emerges from the stars. Your face broken by what you have seen, you place my shoes at the foot of my limp body; you don't look at me.

You leave. My ears ring with my mute scream.

I know I will never see you again. I feel my body sinking slowly underground.

A bunch of us go out to a bar to celebrate the birthday of one of our mutual friends. I go, hoping that you'll come too.

At first, I'm optimistic. I drink a lot, I yak away. Every second I tell myself that you could come in the door, and I turn around fairly often, each time to note your absence.

An hour before closing time. The server offers us the contents of the popcorn machine, which she is getting ready to clean. Completely wasted, I sit on the floor with a giant bowl between my legs and start to cry.

"He didn't come! He didn't come! He hates me!"

A friend sits with me. He tries his best to make me feel better.

"There's still an hour left, maybe he'll join us a bit later. That's his style, to just show up when you're not expecting him."

The hour goes by. You never arrived. My friend and I empty the machine, our mouths obstinately crunching through the kernels. I have never eaten so much popcorn in my life.

I wake up on an inflatable mattress in the middle of an unfamiliar basement, my mouth and throat burning. The artificial flavour of salted butter filling my mouth. A bit of morning daylight comes in through the vertical blinds, which rattle noisily against each other; the sound is unbearable. I am clammy, greasy, damp. My friends are asleep around me on the linoleum. I feel like shouting and startling them awake.

You didn't come. I knew you wouldn't.

I observe the network of twisting pipes on the ceiling above my head, hypnotized by its complexity. The pipes could explode right now, break and send their dirty water down on our bodies stretched out here on the floor.

My eyeliner has run, and I forgot my makeup bag. Bacon, sausages, eggs, sunny-side-up, hash browns, pancakes, ham. We're at the restaurant, sitting around a brunch of cholesterol, and I have nothing to say. Nothing to eat either. Nobody asks me a single question. Everyone else is laughing and rehashing the events of the previous evening. They forget about me, and that suits me fine.

If I had a gun, I could kill everybody.

·

One day, I can't hold out any longer. I dial your number. Your mother is the one who answers and tells me, "Just a second" with a smile in her soft voice. During this second, I rip out a cuticle with my teeth.

You pick up the phone. My words spill out: I tell you I'm an idiot, a real idiot, I never wanted that, I don't get it, the other guy meant nothing, and I'm *so* pissed off at myself.

You say, "That's too bad, I wish — "

In other words, it's too bad that it happened.

Then, we go on talking about this and that, meaningless stuff. As if nothing had happened. About your party for the start of the fall semester at university, about my Cégep courses, about Heath Ledger's death.

At the end of the conversation we say "Bye." Not "See you soon." Not "See you next time."

It's really over. The streetlamp sizzles at the window, and I want to throw stones at it until it bursts. My finger is bleeding all over the phone.

I am so sick and tired of everything, of me, of my body that is just too much.

At lunch, I discover that if I have a green salad without dressing, along with a clementine, I no longer feel anything for the rest of the day. I float, weightless, right above my body.

In class, I find myself newly, and incredibly focused. For the first time in my life, I feel extremely intelligent. I sign up at the gym, where I turn into a warrior. I do two hours on the elliptical machines and an hour of weight training every day. I allow myself an extra clementine after these efforts.

In my head, as in my stomach, a void expands, a void that feels calming, and delectable. Nothing bothers me anymore. All my desires die at the same time as my hunger. A great sense of peace begins to take their place. Everything becomes simpler. With each week that goes by, I find my way back to what is essential.

A month of purification. My brain calms down, but stays alert. I begin to be alone with my mind. Like an ebbing tide, the noise of the world grows farther and farther away, muted. I go deep into a cave I no longer wish to leave.

In the morning, the sun begins to creep between my thighs and comes to strike the wall across from the bed. A marvelously encouraging sight. Like my cheeks, which are sunken now, giving me a more wistful face, more beautiful too.

LIGHTNESS

One day, my skeleton pokes through the surface of my skin. It expresses my state of purity, finally reveals my inner strength. I meticulously wash it, eliminate its impurities, sharpen its contours and its clean, minimal lines. I begin an excellent bone maintenance regimen, with impressive results.

People compliment the healthy maintenance of my neat bones.

I think you would find me beautiful.

You're always there, looking at me. Especially when I jog in the street to burn off my breakfast. I think of you, of your light eyes that go right through me.

I imagine that you're watching me run, as if that was all you had to do. I so wish you could see my bones.

I continue the purification of my life. For the sake of consistency, I decide to rid myself of my possessions. I only want to keep what I absolutely need.

First, I invite my friends over and ask them to empty my room. They find this weird, but they help me get rid of stuff. I sell the rest of my things in front of our house, a sort of garage sale that gives me exactly twelve dollars and forty-five cents. I only keep a few books, some stuffed animals, and my cello.

Next, I repaint my room Bétonel white and hang light cur-

I am so sick and tired of everything, of me, of my body that is just too much.

At lunch, I discover that if I have a green salad without dressing, along with a clementine, I no longer feel anything for the rest of the day. I float, weightless, right above my body.

In class, I find myself newly, and incredibly focused. For the first time in my life, I feel extremely intelligent. I sign up at the gym, where I turn into a warrior. I do two hours on the elliptical machines and an hour of weight training every day. I allow myself an extra clementine after these efforts.

In my head, as in my stomach, a void expands, a void that feels calming, and delectable. Nothing bothers me anymore. All my desires die at the same time as my hunger. A great sense of peace begins to take their place. Everything becomes simpler. With each week that goes by, I find my way back to what is essential.

A month of purification. My brain calms down, but stays alert. I begin to be alone with my mind. Like an ebbing tide, the noise of the world grows farther and farther away, muted. I go deep into a cave I no longer wish to leave.

In the morning, the sun begins to creep between my thighs and comes to strike the wall across from the bed. A marvelously encouraging sight. Like my cheeks, which are sunken now, giving me a more wistful face, more beautiful too.

One day, my skeleton pokes through the surface of my skin. It expresses my state of purity, finally reveals my inner strength. I meticulously wash it, eliminate its impurities, sharpen its contours and its clean, minimal lines. I begin an excellent bone maintenance regimen, with impressive results.

People compliment the healthy maintenance of my neat bones.

I think you would find me beautiful.

You're always there, looking at me. Especially when I jog in the street to burn off my breakfast. I think of you, of your light eyes that go right through me.

I imagine that you're watching me run, as if that was all you had to do. I so wish you could see my bones.

I continue the purification of my life. For the sake of consistency, I decide to rid myself of my possessions. I only want to keep what I absolutely need.

First, I invite my friends over and ask them to empty my room. They find this weird, but they help me get rid of stuff. I sell the rest of my things in front of our house, a sort of garage sale that gives me exactly twelve dollars and forty-five cents. I only keep a few books, some stuffed animals, and my cello.

Next, I repaint my room Bétonel white and hang light curtains on my windows. I put a few pieces of driftwood in a big clay pot. Everything becomes clean and pure, like me. My room looks like a tiny Zen garden. My room like my body, and vice versa.

·

My cello playing becomes more accurate, my movements smoother. I practise like never before. My teacher notices.

For the first time, I'm proud of something. My mind is growing sharper and increasingly honed at the same time as my body.

·

My friends keep telling me I have to forget about you and move on. That I should find some kind of activities to take my mind off you, by which they mean activities commonly known as dates. This is not my strong point. I sign up with a Nature Group at Cégep to accelerate the process.

The first time I go, a guy notices me. His eyes are the same blue as yours, but smaller and more deep-set. He's four years older than me, with canoe-camping muscles. I find him attractive. We chat by ourselves in a corner, away from the others, under the kayak that hangs over our heads.

The afternoon is coming to an end, and he offers to drive me home. I tell him that I live a five-minute walk from the Cégep, at my parents' house, but he repeats his offer. In his car he has me listen to some music by a garage-folk band he has just discovered. He tells me it would be great to see each other again to "continue our discussion" and hands me a post-it with his phone number, as if it was a business card. Gentleman that he is, he waits until I have safely entered my house before starting his engine again and driving off.

My mother, who was watching at the window, asks, "Who was that? He looks a bit old."

I answer that he just offered to drive me home from my climbing course, because he's nice.

As I open Facebook, his friendship request is already there. His wall is plastered with pictures of landscapes and of pixelated wolves on which he's added quotes like, "Life is an adventure." I tell myself he seems okay. Dull, but okay.

•

It isn't yet the start of spring, nor the end of winter. Late one night, the Wolf calls me to go for a walk on the bicycle path. I'm not exactly busy, alone in my basement, but I know that my parents would forbid me from going out so late.

I climb out my bedroom window. I leave it slightly open so that I can get back in later. I crawl under my parents' bedroom window, then walk quickly towards the sidewalk. The empty street echoes with my steps. I have one of those urges to pee, like when I was little and I played hide-and-seek, or when I was doing something naughty.

I turn onto the bike path. The Wolf is there, under the fir tree, watching me with his hunter's gaze. A smile reveals his shiny teeth. Suddenly, he grabs my ass. I don't say anything, I can't say anything anymore because his tongue is already on mine. Anyway, I wouldn't know what to say.

We walk with a steady stride all the way to the marina, where the stink of polluted water makes us keel over in disgust. He compliments my hair, showers my face with praise. I'm not listening. The only thing I feel is the cold; the more he sucks the blood out of me, the more the cold invades me. The stillness here on the docks gives me the impression of moving forward in a dream.

Then, clouds move apart, unveiling the Wolf's face, with his deeply veined forehead. He throws me down on the rocks. No time to protest. With one hand, he unbuttons my skirt, and with the other, he roots around in my mouth. His hand tastes like ass and onions.

I scream at him to stop. Too late. He can't hear anything anymore, will not look at anything except his penis, which he thrusts toward me like an offering. His voice hisses at my ear.

"I know you've been wanting it. This is what you want. I know it."

It's too late. My bare stomach meets the warmth of his. Smoke emanates from this back and this head, from this massive body; it rises into the black sky.

No, it's not too late. I push him away with all the strength I can muster in my legs. He falls, far in front of me, on top of a boulder. His penis in the air. He looks at me with his narrow eyes, astonished. He doesn't understand. I say no. He packs his penis away.

Out of politeness, he walks me home, in complete silence and perfect awkwardness. It seems to get colder. He leaves me there, in front of the house. The player leaves without a new notch on his belt.

In the yard, I climb up to my window, which I find closed. The light is on and my bed is unmade: they've discovered my absence. The number three shines on the alarm clock. Frozen, I no longer feel my body, nor my heart, nor anything else.

I resign myself to my walk of shame.

I go around the house and knock at the front door: three barely audible little taps. My father opens the door immediately. His face is mummified with fatigue. He says, "I heard you go through the gate; we'll talk about it tomorrow."

I go down to my bedroom, where I don't fall asleep. I'm both guilty and relieved, but especially satisfied to have burned enormous quantities of calories during this nocturnal escapade. Adrenaline rushes require a lot of calories; it's been proven. So does the cold.

·

I don't talk about it. I will never talk about it. I tuck it away somewhere and don't touch it again.

·

Choosing an elective is easy, as a nutrition course is available. I'm already an expert on this subject.

The final assignment consists of keeping a food diary and of including all the nutritional and caloric benefits. I'm particularly proud of my methodical, airy journal, with the columns I've traced with a ruler. My caloric total is especially promising.

I only obtain a passing mark. The teacher writes a comment: "Sloppy; incomplete. Is it possible that you have forgotten to list most of your intake?"

·

On the weekend I start riding my bike around Saint Lambert, just in case I run into you. I tell myself that each street could be yours. At the same time, I don't know how I would react if we found ourselves face to face. I don't know if I'd be able to speak.

·

I dig in for the long haul.

Every day I examine your Facebook page, which never changes, in the hope of seeing a sign meant for me. I know all your activities, your rare photos, the even rarer pages that you've liked. I like them too, to attract your attention.

·

Once, only once, I play The Sims to create our avatars and have them meet each other. Yours looks quite a bit like you, and mine does too, except that my Sims does not want to have anything to do with you at first. I have to use a code to make them like each other. I build them a two-storey, red brick house and marry them in their garden with a buffet, a cake and all the bells and whistles. They don't take too long to produce a kid.

The truth is that playing The Sims is more depressing than anything else.

·

I read *Moderato Cantabile* on the lawn chair in my backyard as the magnolias explode into blossom. This is my first time reading Duras. I feel I completely understand everything.

I become Anne Desbaresdes. I stick a branch of flowers in my hair when I go to class.

For some reason, spring is the season that has always depressed me the most. When everything unfurls and fills with colour, I'm overwhelmed by a confusing sense of despair.

This spring, like Anne, I wish someone would kill me.

·

I've never worked. I have to find a job.

Dressed in a new black-and-white striped blouse with a sash

that emphasizes my small waist, I apply at the perfume shop at Place Longueuil. The blonde manager is there, and she takes my c.v. She has me follow her into the back of the store, and I know it's in the bag.

The next day, I make a list of all the products and their ingredients, which I learn by heart. I want to impress her with my professionalism.

When will you stop haunting me?

My mind empties.

There is just this knot, stuck here, blocking my throat. A piece of my heart, still beating a little, against my windpipe. A tough chunk of ventricle. The hardest thing is that I still have his taste in my mouth. This horrible heart that refuses to move on, and makes me so dull and vapid. I so wish I could spit it out. It's of no use to me anyway, except to make me feel this shame and uneasiness, feel this constant, latent nausea caused by my mistake, that night that I betrayed you, that I lost you.

I don't realize it right away, but I finally reach my goal. My periods stop. I hope this is permanent. My periods have ended. Finally free of blood, of leaks, of backaches and bloating. I never thought it would happen: I'm free.

The open window lets in spring and its scent of magnolia. I fall asleep in the boiling water. For a second, I forget my heaviness, my thighs, which are still too fat.

I'm eighteen today and I couldn't care less. I wish I could stay in the bath and disintegrate like the skin on my fingertips. My mother calls me. I get out of the bathtub to dry myself and close the May window. Outside, the sky is beginning a fit of sunshine. Everyone keeps telling me I'm lucky that the weather is so beautiful for my birthday, and it's really getting on my nerves.

Every year my mother brings me to the bakery to choose my cake. As far back as I remember, I have always chosen the dessert dripping with the most calories.

There is one for every taste, according to the fat pastry shop owner. Not for mine, I'm sure. I look, I analyze, and finally just pick one at random. It's all shit anyway, and I have an escape plan.

I eat nothing all day. I'm dizzy; my skull feels like it's imploding. I take a second bath to counter the cold that is invading me again. I isolate myself on my island, under the burning winds of my interior archipelago.

Eighteen candles are lined up on the counter. My mother is preparing the meal. I am fascinated and anxious. There's going to be a lot of food. On birthdays and at celebrations you always have to eat more, to live longer. It's a tradition. My mother smiles at me. I move away from the kitchen. I can already feel the fat thickening on my thighs.

It's suppertime. Faced with this vast heap of food, I hardly eat, just nibble a little here and there in a state of panic. A crumb or two, no more. The whole family watches me picking at my food like a scatterbrained pigeon. I say that I'm saving space for the cake.

My mother expresses her disdain for my behaviour with a harsh glare. My refusal dishonours her. I am unworthy of her and of all that life offers me.

I blow out the candles, forgetting to make a wish. I hide huge bites of cake in my cheeks so that I can spit them out later in my napkin as I wipe my lips. Some sugar crystals stuck to my palate fill my eyes with tears.

At the perfume shop, my manager and her assistant arrive singing Happy Birthday with a package from the pastry shop. I open the box. It's a fruit tart. Panicked, I eat a strawberry from the top to make them happy. Thank you, how nice of you. My reaction disappoints them; they were expecting to see me take a nice big, greedy bite.

I bring the tart home and give it to my brother, who happily gobbles it up in two bites.

I begin to sleepwalk. At night, I walk around the house, from one room to another. I look for someone or something, muttering I don't know what. My parents always end up waking up and bringing me back to my bed. The next day, I don't remember anything.

My only fear is that one night I will get up, go to the cupboard or to the fridge, and carry out the dreaded deed.

.

Another guy from the Nature Group calls me. I consider withdrawing my number from the telephone list.

He invites me out to a restaurant that same night. It's already five in the afternoon. My stomach churns; I can hear a cry of doom in its anguished gurgling. It's tempting to turn him down, so easy to say no. I have no interest in spending an evening stuffing myself while pretending to enjoy it.

He waits politely for my answer on the other end of the line. I know that he can hear my indecision. I quickly accept, only to immediately regret it.

I drift through the next three hours, make return trips between the mirror and the stationary bicycle, meticulously plucking my eyebrows and purging my stomach. I dream about the ideal meal, one with the least sauce, fat, pastry or breadcrumbs. I dream of a soup made of rose petals and clouds. Three hours on the bike, while my eyebrows become two almost invisible lines.

I don't look at him as we get in his car. *Him,* this person I hardly know, who smells like mint and is looking at me with a fresh new gaze. I only have one thing on my mind: where am I being taken? He doesn't speak, and I grow impatient. Smiling a little, he tells me that he wants to surprise me. I hate him. He finally parks and opens my door to let me out. He holds my hand as we walk to the restaurant; I'm like a slave being led to the pillory.

Everything is just amazing. The scent of expensive perfume and clear wine floats in the air. A delicateness far removed from the violence of my imagination.

A Japanese restaurant, that was the surprise. I admit to him that it was a great idea, and kneel at the table. Sushi rolls are false friends, starchy and made of rice, but easily eliminated with a bit of dexterity.

He orders us a platter, the most expensive on the menu. It's still considered romantic to pig out as a couple. Love is a random pretext to binge eat.

The pressure is mounting. They place the monster on the table, under our noses. The curtain rises. It's show time. I grab a random sushi roll, pretend to slip it between my lips, but instead, with admirable agility, drop it into my palm and then under the table. I keep this masquerade going as long as I can; I feign delighted chewing and utter convincing little murmurs of appreciation.

The last sushi roll gone, he reaches across the table to give me a gift bag and, *perhaps* accidentally, drops it on the ground. An anvil falls in my stomach. He pulls the tablecloth up to retrieve the package and then freezes. I know what he sees. I hear his voice, hushed, like a sentence. One word resounds, one word that neatly describes my entire being: disgusting.

Sushi never called me back.

My family takes a trip to the seaside. I stay in the suburbs to work. My parents leave me alone with myself, locked up with an ogress who claws at the fridge, hesitating between emptying it or destroying it.

Eat well, my mother told me. This phrase alone makes me lose my appetite. I know I'll vacillate between paradise and hell, between my dream of having the freedom of eating nothing, of filling myself up on dense sunshine and cool water, and my nightmare of no longer having anyone there to force me to ingest any food whatsoever.

I put the entire contents of both the fridge and the cupboard into a garbage can, then burst into sobs as I hear the garbage truck go by.

·

Under the urban sun, I prepare myself a spectacular case of skin cancer. My oiled skin makes the lines of my bones all the more striking. I am, above all, an exhibitionist. I want to be noticed, to be admired.

Towards the end of the afternoon, I'm suddenly very hungry. I want an apple. No, just a few bites, the rest in the garbage. The minimum, to make my stomach quiet down. I feel like an apple, but I don't want to pay for it. A few cents for food, for something so low, is already too much. I don't have any money to waste.

I enter a hyper-air-conditioned grocery store. The clerk sends smiles my way; an old woman grimaces as she observes my legs. I come to the rows of fruits and vegetables, where Gala apples are regally arranged.

I glance around. The coast is clear. In one swift movement, I grab the reddest piece of fruit and stuff it into my bag. I immediately head to the exit, taking care not to walk too fast. I go through the check-out aisle and the manager calls to me. My heart turns to ice. The old woman is standing right behind him like a vulture.

"Miss. Your bag, please."

Trapped, I hold my bag out to him. He empties it on the counter. The stolen apple falls with a heavy thud. The manager gives me a look that pulls tears from my eyes.

"Give me your parents' phone number. I'm going to advise them to keep an eye on their daughter."

.

After work, in the afternoon, I go around the boutiques. I test tons of make-up, douse myself with all the perfumes. Clothes pile up in the back of the change rooms as I caress, between two sweaters, my beautiful, striking ribs. I have a hole in my torso, digging into my solar plexus.

I don't buy anything, not even my bus tickets.

.

My parents come home and find the cupboard bare. I tell them that there was an invasion of ants, like every summer, and that everything was contaminated. The doubt is dramatically evident on their tanned faces.

A little later, I hear my father shout, "Even in the fridge?"

.

At the start of the new semester I try out for a theatre troupe. I forget my lines, mess up my audition, but am recruited anyway. I have always wondered what short circuit took place in the director's brain the moment he made that decision.

The script of this play is pretty heavy. I only have a few lines, and I'm incapable of memorizing them. My brain deletes the sentences as I go along.

I find myself in a story within a story that makes me dizzy, because I play a role which plays a role on top of the one I continually play in real life. I don't sound convincing. They tell me that over and over. Sometimes, I *do* sound convincing. During a few moments of clarity when I forget myself, when I just let go. Like when I faint.

It's my mother's birthday. The guests are packed into the living room and they fill their plates with tapas while pretending to have conversations, their mouths slow and awkward. They don't know anything anymore, they don't remember why they're over at our house. There is food here for them and that's all.

I watch them from my corner and curse their drops of sweat; I am completely numb with cold. I feel like screaming and making them freeze between two bites, so they can see themselves and the outrageousness of their behaviour.

I observe them from above, from afar, with my crooked gaze, superior. I know that I don't look like these animals, and at the same time, I envy their mindlessness.

My godmother comes close to me. She seems worried about how I look.

"Are you sick?"

"No, I'm just cold."

I swing her an enormous smile so that she leaves me alone. In general, we don't really feel like talking much when we're freezing to death. It's a sort of economy of language, a survival tactic so that all our energy remains focused on getting warm.

When my mother tells me that my lips are blue, I break down and head to the bathroom.

The face reflected in the mirror is indecent. White, yellow and blue, with red eyes circled in grey. My face looks like a mask, carved with a knife, with its sunken cheeks and concave temples.

I turn on the hot water tap — and not the cold — peel off the three woolen layers I've been wearing and then finally enter the giant kettle. My body relaxes and my bones crack.

Someone's knocking on the door. My mother's voice.

"Is anyone in there?"

"Yes, me. I'm taking a bath."

"Another bath? We're waiting for you, for the cake!"

More than ever before, I want to weld myself to the porcelain under my ass, dissolve and get sucked down the drain to go join the life that is waiting for me, over there, at the other end of the tunnel.

My head is shattering. Why don't you just eat your fucking cake, you bunch of pigs, and leave me the fuck alone?

But I answer simply, obediently.

"I'm coming, Mom."

·

Once, I stalk you on Facebook and come across a photo of you standing close to a girl, your arms touching. Laughing. A *chick*. I cry all evening, all night. The next day, I tell myself that she might be just a friend. According to your profile information you're still single. I'm counting on that, anyway.

·

For an outdoor activity course at Cégep, somewhere up north, I hover on snowshoes over two metres of snow. The pine trees encircle me like a ghostly army. I turn around and watch the other students struggling at the bottom of the hill, sinking into the snow with each step, stumbling.

I'm strong, like the sun beating down on my head. My legs, sheathed in my tights, are like those of the deer I came across earlier. I am a perfectly adapted animal, programmed for survival.

As the teacher catches up to me, he exclaims, "What did you eat this morning that's making you go so fast?"

Nothing. In fact, that's exactly what I've eaten. Nothing.

The boys stop to pee. I keep going, opening the path. As soon as someone gets close to me, I pick up speed. I want to be alone in this performance, in this feat.

The frozen lake lies in front of me. I can see the water flowing in the shallows.

We take a break. I unwrap my sandwich, just eat the tomatoes, wrap it back up. Enough, it's already too much. I stuff the bread in my bag and continue on my way.

In the back, I hear people murmuring about me. I imagine that the lake's surface is vibrating and that we're sinking into white water. I find this idea relaxing.

Around the end of the afternoon, the sun goes down before our eyes. The group is collapsing, far behind, incapable of going any further. The teacher suggests I keep going up to the cabin by myself to light the fire while the others rest.

My silhouette glides over valleys and hills, squeezes between the branches and rocks. Suddenly, it's nighttime. The creatures observe me and bow to me as I go by. I'm one of them. Antlers grow through my tuque, and I can feel a coat of fur bristling on my back. My eyes pierce the polar night.

I reach the drafty old cabin. I have a miserable time trying to light the fire with wet newspapers. The lighter falls from my petrified hands and breaks on the brick floor. I look for matches in the mouldy drawers; I find none. There are the ghosts of trappers around me, standing in each corner of the room. One sitting on the chair next to the stove. His breath overwhelms me, pushes my whole body down on the papers. As I fall, my antlers scratch the ground and are scuffed.

Hard fingernails dig into my ankles. A girl is raising my legs. "She opened her eyes!"

The teacher puts me down on the closest bed. A bit of low blood pressure, he explains. Just eat a bowl of spaghetti and everything will be okay. I refuse, claiming to feel too sick to eat anything. He doesn't insist.

Reverberating laughter. The students party in the wood, flirt and drink beer.

And then I don't hear anything anymore. The ghost by the stove comes and lies down in the bed and puts his arms around me. I feel his glacial embrace against my skin, against my bones, and I imagine winter talking to me through the crack in the back wall.

·

During a rehearsal, a girl from the troupe comes to see me:

"Hey, you've lost a lot of weight. Are you okay?"

"I'm having a really busy semester, I'm tired, that's all. Don't worry about me."

That's what I say to my family, to my friends. Don't worry. Even if everybody is worrying a little.

·

I make an appointment with the shrink at Cégep. I'm allowed a maximum of three visits. As I sit down in her office, I don't know how to act. I'm mesmerized by a Turner print on the wall: a ship in a storm, a little dot lost in a monochromatic blue-grey.

The shrink with the buzzcut turns her chair towards mine. Her pen suspended over my file, she asks what's brought me here.

"Well, I think I might have some problems with food."

Her small, watery eyes appraise me from over her square glasses.

"With food? Funny, what *I* see in front of me is a young woman who seems athletic, fit. What makes you think you have an eating disorder?"

And she lowers her eyes; writing incredibly quickly, she notes my response.

"Um, I don't know, it takes up a lot of space in my thoughts, I think, my body, I mean."

"Well, you know, with all the peer pressure, fashion, and advertising, it's normal at your age to be preoccupied with your appearance. But actually, you seem to be at a healthy weight. You shouldn't worry about it. Did you experience a traumatic event recently?"

"No, never."

"You must be going through a stressful period right now. How are your courses going, and your semester?"

The hour allocated to me seems interminable. I won't use my two other appointments. I don't need to, as I've already received my professional diagnosis; I don't have any problems. Except the fact that I'm not skinny enough yet.

·

I learn that the Wolf has died. Apparently, he hanged himself at home. They say he didn't leave anything behind.

·

Nothing's going right with the cello anymore. I've lost my sound. My teacher won't stop nagging me about it. Push into the string, use your weight. I can't. I hold back tears. I give up, put down my bow.

My teacher gets it, maybe more than I think she does. I cancel my future lessons. It's over.

One morning, my father wakes me up. Get up, he says. Some people are here to see you. Get dressed.

He looks serious.

I pull on some clothes and go upstairs. Some police officers are standing at the front door. They ask me my name. Their eyes question me, the way one would silently interrogate a criminal. They say, "Sit down", and I do, struck down by their obscure force. I feel blood and sweat flowing between my legs, between my breasts like a blade.

They say my name. Then his name, the Wolf's. And that he died, on March 20. That they found his body on the shore, his face in the mud, his skull shattered by a fall on the rocks.

"You knew this boy, didn't you?"

"Yes."

"Do you know, by any chance, what he was doing there that night, on the beach?"

"No, no idea."

"Where were you that night?"

"I don't remember."

My father intervenes.

"She was at home, studying. She had an exam to prepare for."

"All right," they say to me. "Thank you. Call us if you have any new information about this." Then they leave. I am too fragile to be a suspect.

It's raining in the garden, on the Wolf's shattered corpse. His penis reaching straight towards the sky, he comes back to life, then goes back to being dead. His accusing eyes fixed on mine, he repeats:

"That's what you always wanted. And it's what you did. I know."

A scream invades my stomach, a huge scream, like his death. Then he closes his little eyes again, leaves me in peace. My father mows the lawn next to me.

I drop to the ground and cover his body with fragrant pine branches. My fingers are sticky with his seminal fluid, with which I embalm my lips. I strike a match and throw it on him. I set his body on fire; it smells good. Everything is over for him. The flames rise all the way into the night to erase the stars. All I have to do now is jump into this blaze myself, burn this worn-out scaffolding that I use as a body. But I don't; I'm too heavy to jump. Like an elephant, the only animal incapable of the slightest jump.

·

I work with the new salesgirl at the perfume shop. A straight-talking sort of girl, no makeup, plump, my antithesis. Her eyes travel the length of my body. She says, "You're so beautiful, so slim. How do you do it?"

Every time someone asks me this question, I answer with a shrug.

"Do you eat well?"

"Yes, I always eat whatever I want. I've got a good metabolism."

My eyelid twitches. No, I don't eat well, and I don't eat much. Just enough to survive, to be able to stand up without my legs trembling, the minimum to be able to open and close the boutique without fainting at some point in between. But you're never going to find out all that.

The girl pushes her plate of vine leaves bathed in olive oil. "Have one," she says. I take an invisible bite so that she leaves me alone.

"Go ahead, have more, I've got tons."

"No thanks, I'm not hungry, I just had lunch."

Her eyes narrow.

We close the boutique. The hallway lights go off. In the gloom of the vacant shopping centre, the boutiques, where everything is on sale, confront each other in silence.

As I pass through the automatic doors, the evening's humidity invades me like a kind of nausea. I know, I lied, it's like a habit for me. I can't help it; it's more powerful than anything else, this voice that comes out of I-don't-know-where to speak over my own objections.

I take a deep breath, hoping to purify myself, but I know that it's in vain. I'm a liar. That's the way it is. Some things are destined to be rotten.

·

I'm lost in an improbable identity zone, buried under successive layers of cheap paint. But I feel that the white is starting to peel away, and that an odour of mould is being released from underneath.

·

I do two theatre school auditions. At both of them, they interrupt my scene after the first minute and thank me for coming. When I receive my rejection letters, I feel absolutely nothing. Almost liberated from a heavy weight, one less role to play.

·

I register for a Bachelor's degree in Literature, almost out of cowardice. I feel that literature will probably be of some use to me, in the long run, like a survival kit, or a sewing kit. It could maybe help me to patch some pieces back together, mend the bits that have been torn. And also, writing is minimal, doesn't take any space, costs nothing. Writing is practical.

.

I'm accepted.

Full of good intentions, I race to borrow the books for my courses in order to begin them during the summer and get a head start. I won't open any of them.

.

For my first trip across the pond, I choose Ireland, my country, kingdom of hunger and strength. At the airport, before I go through customs, my mother orders me to feed myself well.

On the plane I don't eat a thing, and I take advantage of the all-you-can-drink Coke Zero.

.

I land in Dublin. At breakfast at the youth hostel I steal some bread. I eat exactly one slice in the morning with jam and half a slice at noon with a thin sliver of turkey. At night I don't eat anything, or I end up wandering into a bar for a Guinness. Here, my famine makes me feel very Irish, I see things differently, through a special filter, a unique, inner disposition which brings me closer to this land, the rocks and the cliffs, the people buried under foundries, ghosts. The slightest deviation and I fall, or I fly away. I cycle around the coves and mountains. I never stop falling, crashing on the roads. I smash my teeth. I mangle myself, and it's just ecstasy.

I find myself alone on a tiny little island one afternoon, at the edge of a cliff. A half-devoured goat lies dying at my side and stares at me, his eyes mad with supplication. Mesmerized, I can't stop myself from staring back at her, but I don't do anything. I can't leave her either. I have to accompany her, passively, as she dies. It's dusk when the goat finally falls silent. Its delirious bleats will haunt my nights; they will morph into calls for help.

·

Frugal to the extreme, I nick food from hostel fridges and never buy myself anything. I return from Ireland more emaciated than ever, bearing only my thinness as a souvenir.

·

My parents chew me out. I'm sure *you* would find me gorgeous.

·

I become addicted to caffeine, taurine and guarana. My survival depends on Monster, Red Bull, Rockstar, and Guru. Only sugarless for me. I steal money from my parents' change jar, and the first thing I do in the morning is rush to the corner store or the supermarket to celebrate the two-for-one specials. I hoard the empty cans in my closet to avoid alarming my parents with my overconsumption.

I close up the boutique while a guy prowls around outside the door. He starts by watching me from a distance, through the window. I already know what will happen next.

He finally walks in, with a determined stride. Not bad-looking, the tall, blond type, with green eyes, but he's wearing a baseball cap. I pretend to be counting the cash. This does not stop him. "Hey, I've noticed you — for a while now. I work at the liquor store across the mall. You free tonight? Wanna have a drink?"

I say "Yes." "No" would have been the right thing to say, both to prevent me from making myself suffer and also from pissing him off. I don't know why I accept. Maybe to prove that I can still be normal, like everyone else.

I have to finish up closing the shop. The dude watches me as I work; he's already getting on my nerves with his smell of Axe and the gum he's chewing so hard he's about to dislocate his own jaw. Out of his sight in the backstore, I place a drop of perfume on my neck, then turn off the lights.

I let him lead me to his car without even asking him his name, like an old whore who has done this loads of times. It's once I'm buckled into my seat that I pretend to be interested in him. I finally react when he asks me where I want to go. I shrug my shoulders, because a no-calorie bar exists nowhere, not even in my dreams.

He winks at me like a pro and declares, "You love beer. Am I right?"

I answer "Yes." He parks like a cowboy. Then he comes around to open my door, presumably to score a few fuck points.

He goes to the bar and orders two pints and a plate of nachos. His eyes explore me, from head to toe. He says, "You're in pretty good shape." I answer that I go to the gym sometimes. He tells me that he goes too, and I raise an eyebrow despite myself as I turn my gaze from his well-padded belly, a big cushion that he fills with nachos covered with melted cheese and sour cream.

The dude has no self-consciousness. He eats and drinks at a frantic pace. I can't stop myself from imagining him choking. I don't say a word.

At some point, he stops. He realizes that something's wrong.

"You haven't had any beer or natchos."

"No. I'm taking my time."

He bounces back, visibly flattered that I wish to prolong my time in his company. He begins a monologue which is about his job, his gym routine, his friends, his parties, I guess.

I reach toward the plate of nachos. I carefully select a shriveled piece with no cheese. I chew it slowly. Then, with similarly minute movements, I bring my glass of beer to my lips and let a meager millilitre flow into my mouth. I keep this nectar in my mouth for a long time to savour its flavours. Definitely much too good. I tell him, "The beer really is good!" and I don't drink any more.

He urges me to drink. "No," I say, "I have a bit of a stomach ache." He's disappointed. I won't be tipsy enough for him to lure me to his bed tonight. I can see it in his eyes, in the lecherous glint that suddenly disappeared.

To crown it all, the waiter sets a gigantic glass before me, "on the house". He taps his good customer on the shoulder as he goes away.

The dude is starting to get royally pissed off with me, and I don't blame him. He pays; we leave. Fifty bucks for a disastrous evening with a living disaster, a hollow shell. In his car, which weaves in and out of lanes all the way to my house, he doesn't speak. It's here. He doesn't come around to open my door. We exchange a few meaningless words and he vanishes into the night. No kisses, no promises.

In my bedroom, I try to empty my mind. I begin a hundred

sit-ups in the hope of making this evening disappear, the dude, the nachos and the drop of beer.

.

My instrument sits in its dusty corner, watching me with an accusing glare. I haven't touched it for months.

The date of the play is approaching fast and I'm not going over my lines anymore. My brain is on "off," no longer takes in anything from the novels I'm supposed to be reading for my courses.

I don't have the energy to give a fuck about anything whatsoever. I go to bed at nine at the latest. It's all I can before falling into bed, still in my clothes and makeup, my teeth unbrushed.

.

I cross the bridge. Through the wire netting, you can see the water flowing. Like death, which gently flows beneath my skin. Something that's right there that we refuse to look at. I'm already on the other side of the river.

The girls are waiting for me at the waterfront bar. They smell of beer, gush with laughter. I order a glass of water, so I can crush the ice cubes. I freeze my brain. The hairs on my body stand up straight. The girls talk about getting wasted, getting laid, things I don't get, that I can't relate to. I feel alienated from them, from what they're talking about. Their language appalls me. Their lives strike me as foul, filthy, repugnant. I retreat into my own asexual headspace.

My legs rise involuntarily and bring me to the bathroom, with no wish but to escape, if only for a moment.

I have nothing to say to these girls. The only language that works for me emanates from my bones. My bones say it all, express what I want people to see in me. On me. Purity in linear form. Sure, there could always be so much more to say; I *could* speak for hours about this and that. But everything is said, right here, under my skin's surface. My bones.

I think about all of that while I pretend to go pee.

In the meantime, the girls are talking about my weight, I know. I feel it in my back like goosebumps, and I wash my hands of it.

I come back to the table. The moon is high on the other side of the river. The girls order a dessert. I nibble on a salad, with its threatening puddle of oil underneath. The girls don't look at me, the way one avoids looking at a corpse in its coffin. At the end of the meal there is still the ordeal of having to pay for this crappy food. I grit my teeth and take out a ten-dollar bill, throw it on the counter without turning around. It's at least two dollars short.

We leave. The girls are drunk. I keep my mouth shut.

At the corner, in front of the Victorian hotel, a woman is lying on the street, facing the sky. Her huge open eyes do not look at us, as a red trickle escapes from a crack at the top of her head. The girls stop talking. I stop breathing. Police officers suddenly emerge from nowhere and surround the young body with a security cordon. The scene bathes in a silence of fresh blood.

There is nothing to say about death. We cross the river.

.

My first class at university. Something shifts in my ribcage and then gently flutters. I've never felt anything like this before. My heart speeds up. I firmly believe I'm going to die. Right there, like that, in the middle of the lecture, my face stamped on the table and my hair in a small pool of spilled coffee. The death of an old junkie.

I gather all my mental strength to stop myself from dying, but I feel my whole body is deserting me. I stand up, leaving my notebooks, my bag, and my honour behind me. I leave the classroom and go directly to the hospital. The palpitations get stronger and tickle the back of my throat. I see stars. It would be almost pleasant if I weren't so scared. I call my parents.

"Daddy, I'm going to Emergency."

"What?"

"I'm having these big palpitations. I think it's a heart attack."

"All right, I'll come and meet you there."

Chaos in the waiting room. They finally shout my name. The nurse doesn't examine me. In fact, she tells me off instead, in her Romanian accent. You don't come to Emergency when you have palpitations.

She finally says, "Take your shoes off and get on the scales." My feet on the cold metal. I hold my breath while she plays with the weights. Then she measures me and her eyebrows go down when, after putting the two numbers together, the calculator gives her an ambiguous 18.7. "Your BMI is borderline. Watch it."

She goes back to her office, leaving me on the table covered with paper. The palpitations stop. I look at my arms for a long time. I play with their flab, find them repulsive, not thin enough, just borderline. I take the time to thoroughly loathe myself before returning to the jungle.

My father is waiting for me; he's eating peanuts. He gets up, points the bag in my direction and says, "Want some?" I don't even bother answering him. "Your mother's worried. Call her to let her know you're okay."

In my mother's eyes, my thinness is a challenge. No. An attack. Against her, against life. I know, because she narrows her eyes when she looks at me, as if responding to an affront. I won't let you win, she seems to be saying. I don't want an 18-year-old child. Eat, grow taller, get bigger, hurry the fuck up.

She is one of the rare people who know my little secrets, my depraved mind.

I know that when she holds me in her arms, she feels a vague wave of disgust and pity. I know that touching my bones traumatizes her, and that she experiences that feeling whenever she even thinks about me.

On the phone, her voice seems to come up from a grave. "It's not easy, living with you," she tells me. "I've had all I can take of your nonsense. I'm worn out."

·

I find myself fatter than ever. No matter how much weight I lose, my bones are still too big for me to be really delicate. I'm condemned to being "hefty," "big-boned," with a belly that will never go flat. I'm a fake at being skinny, another fucking wannabe. There's nothing convincing about me. I'm just a fucking joke.

·

There's a party with the theatre troupe for the end of the shows. I cycle for three hours, to empty myself. Before I go, I swallow a raw red bell pepper and a large black coffee. The mirror displays my legs, sheathed in pantyhose under my mini-skirt. I'm ready. There's a taste of shit in my mouth.

A stranger opens the door. I go down to the seedy-looking basement, which smells like the bottom of an ashtray. I throw my bag into a space under the staircase. Everyone is already too wasted to notice me, except for one dude I don't know.

He comes over to me, offers me his bottle of Jack Daniels. I'm already a bit unsteady on my legs after a single sip. After two, I tell Jack that I bet I can drink faster than him. "O.K. I want to see that." Two glasses are filled to the top. Everyone starts shouting. As the glass empties, my eyes fill with water, my ears close. I can't hear anything anymore, I don't even know that I won. My fingers drop the glass, which shatters on the carpet.

A minute later, I'm dancing on the roof of a white car. I might be singing too. Then, all of a sudden, my body flips from the inside, like a wet winter glove that is turned inside out. I paint the top of the hood of the car with vomit the colour of a red pepper.

I'm in the bathroom, where two girls are French-kissing, sitting on the ledge of the sink. I continue my purification behind their indifferent backs.

Jack volunteers to bring me home. I probably accept because he's helping me walk. He says, "Give me directions; I don't know the area." I tell him the way, and we get lost.

I start to complain, "I drank too many calories, I have to burn them off now, I'm so ugly and enormous." I say this aloud. He doesn't answer. We walk for what seems like most of the night. Finally, we come to a house with green shutters and I say, "There it is."

Jack disappears. I have no idea if I thanked him or even said goodbye. I'll never see him again.

I collapse on my bed, practically in an alcoholic coma. The next morning, the alarm clock shrieks all the way inside my cerebral cortex. I'm the one who's supposed to open the boutique this morning. As I get up, I puke on my bedroom floor. Then I brush my hair, in which little chunks of red peppers still cling.

My mother drives me to the boutique. She asks me how the party was. I don't answer, too focused on pushing down what is coming up in my throat. The rearview mirror reflects red eyes featuring popped veins, with rings of old mascara underneath.

As the shopping centre opens, I stand in front of the boutique and stare at the lock. My neurons reconnect. The key in my bag, the bag under the stairs, the stairs in that house from last night. I turn on my heels and run after my mother's car, which is driving away.

We pull up in front of the house, passing the white car, which is still stained red. I ring the bell. Nobody answers the door. I ring again. Not a sound. I'm frantic; my whole being is pounding. Anguish overwhelms me. And then I turn the doorknob and the door opens.

The basement is filled with bodies. I retrieve my bag; nobody sees me. I could have made off with a couple of wallets. We return to the boutique, which I open clumsily, my nerves jangling. The phone rings the second I move to my position behind the cash. My boss's cheerful voice asks, "How's it going this morning?"

My tongue is furry, my teeth coated, my breath foul. I tell her everything's going really, really well.

·

I wake up with a start. There's a ghost in the corner of my bedroom. It's the Wolf again, naked, giving me the same vacant look that he'd had on the riverbank. I hate ghosts, especially his. I turn on the light and find myself alone with my roaring stomach.

I know I won't be able to go back to sleep. I toss and turn this endless night; I'm too hungry to sleep. I lie on my stomach to trick myself into believing it is full. I have to fall asleep to get my mind off it.

My body rises and does precisely what I've forbidden it to do. It heads to the kitchen. It wants to fill itself up.

My arms open the cupboard. My hands refuse to take anything at all.

I return to my bed, which has grown cold.

In this hopeless state I get up again and go to the bathroom. I run myself a bath, turning on only the hot water. The steam wraps me in softness, allows me to take in the sensual delight of my skin against this second skin.

My sister enters, squinting, sleepy.

"What the hell are you doing? It's three in the morning."

"I'm about to take a bath."

Unconcerned, she goes back to bed. The fact that she can sleep really pisses me off.

The bath is ready. I slide all the way in and watch my body change colour. The burn is delicious. Time goes by, and I finally doze off. My stomach fills with warmth. I get out hours later, just as I am sinking into a state of inertia. Finally calm, I slip under my blankets and immediately fall asleep. I don't dream about anything. A lovely, restful state of emptiness.

The next day, my sister looks at me, frowning.

"I dreamt about you. It was really fucked up. You were taking a bath in the middle of the night."

"It's not your dream that's fucked up. It's me."

·

Everything's sticky, from the floor to the sweating bodies. The odour of the bar, the people.

I smile and laugh too hard, fake having fun. I go to pee every five minutes, I'm so bored. My friends buy rounds. I drink one beer after another. My belly bloats like an inflatable cushion. Its reflection in the bathroom mirrors petrifies me. I wish I could crush it with my high heels.

On the dance floor I bounce around to burn the calories I've been ingesting. My friends think I'm having the greatest time. They shout in my ears to egg me on. But in my head there is only panic. I must destroy it all, burn it all. Whatever I do, I can't stop. No fun for you, girl. No, absolutely none.

It's my turn to pay a round. Actually, no, go fuck yourselves, everyone. I don't have any money on me. There's an ATM at the back, they tell me. *Fuck.*

I withdraw forty dollars, which turns into six bottles. I'm seething. No tip tonight. To make my rage and my calories go away I dance like I've never danced before, in a kind of frenzy.

The lights finally go back on, and the music stops. I'm saved. We leave and hail a taxi. No, not me. I don't want to pay. Enough is enough. I don't have any money. I have nothing more to give. I collapse on a snow bank. Leave me alone.

Let me live a life with no money, no alcohol, no food and no sex. I don't want to be like you.

My friends pick me up by the armpits and throw me in the taxi. You're coming with us. And you're going to pay, like everyone else.

·

At night, I walk around the house.

I go to the kitchen to pour myself glasses of water and leave the tap on. I yell at my parents because it's too dark and I open the curtains, turn on the lights and the TV. My books turn up on the shelves of the fridge. Every night is different from the one before.

I don't remember anything the next morning. I just feel exhausted as if I had never slept in my whole life. I'm a wreck.

·

I'm alone at home when my arm goes numb and I'm suddenly overwhelmed by the urge to vomit. I'm having a heart attack.

I look up the warning signs on the Internet. Chest pains. Sweats. Discomfort elsewhere in the upper body. Shortness of breath. Nausea. Dizzy spells. If you experience any of these symptoms, you must DIAL 9-1-1 or your local emergency number immediately.

A chill settles on my back like a thin layer of frost. A vise tightens around my chest, crushing it.

I slip; I grab the wall. The feeling of slowly sinking, like before falling asleep. What is happening to me? I slap myself in the face to bring myself back. My hands, my feet and my heart are shaking uncontrollably, violently. I am so confused and upset by how they shake against my will. My scream penetrates the whole empty house.

I get up, grab the cordless phone, dial 911 and give them my address. I ask them to turn off the ambulance lights and sirens to avoid alarming the neighbours.

I stagger toward the sink, turn the tap all the way on and swallow about twenty glasses of water.

The doorbell rings. I open the door to the nurses, who bring me to the ambulance, where they probe me with their hands, check my pulse, my blood pressure, and my breathing. Everything's stable, they tell me. Apparently, I'm not at risk of dying. They notice that my limbs are trembling and conclude, "You're probably having a panic attack. Eat something, and get some rest."

The ambulance leaves in silence and I go back into the house. My heart goes back to its normal rhythm. I pee for three minutes straight.

When my parents come home from work, I don't tell them anything.

Later, when it's time to go to sleep, I have to leave my light on. My phone must be near my bed, within my reach. I put on the Harry Potter soundtrack, on low volume.

I don't want to fall asleep, because I won't wake up. I can feel death hovering near my body and know that it's just waiting for a moment of inattention to capture this empty shell.

I sleep, and it passes.

·

I cut out the energy drinks, but also coffee, tea, chocolate and sugar. My withdrawal migraine lasts over a week.

·

I invited you over for my nineteenth birthday party. Not directly, of course, but through a Facebook event.

Almost all my friends are here. They try to get me to drink and I consistently refuse. I have to stay sober this time. The clock seems strangely still. I deign to dance a little, just to make the time pass.

I can only think of one thing. Are you coming? I invited you, although I was quite aware that it was a stupid, useless move. You didn't even answer the invitation, not even with a "maybe". But we never know, sometimes…

Around midnight, I sink into an armchair with a glass of ice cubes. Seeing my face, the girls surround me and take my hands. I begin to cry, repeating, "He didn't come, he didn't come." The evening's not over yet, they tell me, rolling their eyes.

It's too much for me, too much noise, too many people, too many disappointments. Without a word, I go downstairs to my room and get in bed.

The next day, I wake up with a horrible sensation on my skull. I touch my hair, which is sticky and smells like lemons. I don't get it. I notice a can of my father's shaving cream at the foot of my bed and swear to myself that I will never have another party.

After washing my hair three times, I check my emails. I almost do have a heart attack when I see the bold letters indicating a new message. A message from you. I click to open it and the computer decides to freeze, at that exact moment. I chew the fingernail of my middle finger right down to the cuticle, where it hurts. The email opens a few minutes later.

Hi,

Just wanted to let you know that I came to your house yesterday around one in the morning, but it looked empty and the lights were off...? I rang the bell and nobody answered...?

Anyway, happy belated birthday...

.

Two days. It takes me two days before I can answer your email. I don't know what to write; I don't want to fuck up again. I weigh every one of my words. I open my email in the morning, prepare to write to you, stay blocked for ten minutes in front of the screen, then close the page and move away from the computer. I'll read it later. Except that taking so long to answer is also starting to look a bit suspicious.

Finally, I opt for a pseudo-confident, direct style that could never turn against me, whatever happens. I end it with an invitation to meet me the following Saturday and rush to click "Send" before I can change my mind.

.

You answer me the same evening. I'm crying as I open the message.

"Saturday works for me."

My hands are trembling with hunger, exhaustion and hope. On my bike the whole day, intoxicated by the sun's rays.

Freed from my body, flying away, soaring on the bridge, glorious. I don't worry about anything anymore, not even the incoherence of my thoughts, not even the palpitations hammering my chest. I'm lifted up by the immensity of the sky.

Below, the horizon pulls away. I'm ablaze in this light; I pedal like a machine.

The sun hides behind the city.

I wait for you on the terrace, by the river. A blue shimmer in the night. You appear. The idea that I'd see you again was so improbable. Something spreads open inside me when you smile at me again, for the second time.

We go in. I sit down and so do you. Your eyes stare at my neck, at my collarbones. We shoot the crap; we meander around, get lost together in our conversation. I tell you about my trip to Ireland. You tell me that you love Ireland. You drink. I drink because you do. We empty a pitcher. A bitter, acidic flower rises in my esophagus and my belly howls its loathing.

I disturb you. The sight of my neck rattles you. I know what you think of me. I sense it in the way you look at me. You can tell. You can read it on my stretched cheeks, and my ribs, visible at the edge of my neckline. You know how to read my bones, and I'm ashamed of them, now that you can see them.

We stop talking.

You take my hands the way people do with a dying person, and your warmth causes my purplish fingers to crack. I don't know what to do.

I want to tell you that, since the summer I turned seventeen, my nights have been literally restless and my dreams devoid of meaning, love and sex.

But I don't say anything about that. Instead I say, "I have to go home."

The houses and trees spin around us. You ride back with me on your bike. I'm reeling, drunk on sunshine, alcohol and you. I tell you about my sleepwalking; I've been wearing my agitated nights on my face for months now. I'm a little ghost haunting the house, that house over there. White with green shutters, do you see where it is?

You tell me:

"Yes, that's where I rang the doorbell for your birthday party the other day. How come nobody was there?"

"The party ended early."

In front of my house, you lift me, too easily. I let myself fall and tumble with you onto the asphalt.

You step back, with shattered eyes, like the last time. You say:

"You're so skinny."

"It's not me, I mean, it's not my fault."

I don't add anything else. One day, maybe, I will decide to tell you everything. But that day is far away.

·

I'm here on earth like in heaven, but heaven isn't really such a peaceful place. I'm constantly afraid of falling. I know that you're still mad at me, that you distrust me, so I do my best, retreat behind the image of the perfect girlfriend.

I've never felt less concrete.

I meet your family. Your parents have just come back from Spain; they cook a paella. I separate the vegetables from the rice, push aside the starches, the meats. I don't finish the food on my plate. My stomach is still too full at the end of the meal, and I'm drunk on a corrosive sort of Grappa.

We go down to your bedroom and we make love for the first time. I don't get it. I'd replayed the scene hundreds of times, united our bodies with passion in my head. But now that you take me in your arms, I remain passive, limp. I don't feel anything, or maybe just a vague wish to kiss you, as if you were a Prince Charming without a body, just a lovely head, like on those posters for teens. A little girl's desire. Distraught, I cry into your neck when your forehead finally drops onto my shoulder.

I don't know how to act; I'm not subtle enough. You bring me snacks I never feel like eating, you buy me chocolates I hide in my clothes. You spin your wheels while I back away, withdraw into my shell.

You don't understand when I tell you that I don't want anything.

My cello hasn't been tuned in ages. It sits under mountains of dust. I dream of selling it so that it will stop staring at me.

While I'm doing housework one day, I bump into it with my knee. I hear its sound post cracking. A crack of dead wood. The belly is suddenly flattened; the cello collapses on itself, implodes.

It's damaged beyond repair. I don't know how to dispose of it. I save its corpse in its black case and shove it to the back of my closet.

I'll never play for you.

·

I'm afraid my parents will open my closet.

·

Everyone's asleep.

A bag of popcorn is lying on the counter. I rip it open and devour it by fistfuls. The bag is already empty.

Insatiable, I open the refrigerator door. Six grapefruit lie on a tray right in front of my nose. I wolf down the first one without removing the peel. I sit on the floor, the juice spraying my eyes, running down my chin, between my breasts. Then I eat the other five. A sticky lake forms, composed of spit and juice. I get down and lick up the little puddle.

I lower my head as I wipe my mouth and notice an enormous roll of flesh spilling over my waistband.

I go to the mirror and see: padded arms, sagging breasts, an unrestrained abdomen and undefined cheeks. My head spins. I crush the little cellulite bumps on my thighs and an oily substance oozes from some wounds.

My dripping legs smell like melted butter.

I start puncturing all the swollen bubbles that compose this disastrous body. The smell of grease makes me sick, and I throw up the entire contents of my stomach, which is so brutally shaken up after several spasms that it begins to liquidate my internal organs. I easily identify the liver, the pancreas, the small and large intestines, the kidneys. I insert a finger into the back of my throat. With a delicious convulsion, I vomit my uterus and Fallopian tubes.

I feel incredibly relieved. I'm thin and gorgeous again.

·

I run to the river, and then the length of the marina. I turn back to take a shower, exhausted and serene.

On the way home, I feel my throat squeezing itself, like a vacuum-sealed bag. Piercing pain in my heart.

I slow down. Take my pulse, which is abnormally fast and strong. I walk home, tell myself it's probably nothing, it will pass.

It doesn't pass.

My sister is making herself toast. A surge of adrenalin overwhelms me as I open the fridge. I'm a rocket taking off. I sit down in the living room, breathe, take my pulse, do not faint.

It still doesn't go away.

My arms and my legs start to tremble, slightly at first, and then violently. I walk around and around the armchair in a frenzy. My sister watches me and realizes that something's up.

"I feel ... not well, really not well. I think I'm going to call the Health Hotline."

I dial 811. "Please note that in order to ensure better service, your call will be recorded."

The nurse seems worried about me.

"Have you exerted yourself recently?"

"I just went running. That's when I started to feel bad."

The line crackles and then a different woman's voice comes on.

"Miss, this is 911, your symptoms are very worrying. We're sending you an ambulance right now. What is your address?"

My condition gets worse, degenerates. I'm going to die, right here, right now. I think about you, whom I'll never see again. I have nothing better to do, so I concentrate on the pages of an IKEA brochure lying by the telephone. The people in the pictures laugh as they wash dishes; they are completely unconcerned by death. I try to project myself into their life to slow down my demise while waiting for the ambulance.

When it arrives, I make my sister get in with me.

I order the driver to hurry up and start the engine. My limbs no longer tremble; they are literally whipping the air with erratic movements, like those of an epileptic. Once we're on the road, the paramedics listen to my chest. Your heart's beating very fast, they tell me.

I look out the window. Chambly Road is going by too slowly, with its succession of dissimilar buildings, outdated logos, unisex hair salons, pizzerias with burned-out neon signs, run-down sex shops. The same route my mother probably took twenty years ago to give birth to me. I'm going in the opposite direction. Birth and death on Chambly Road.

I scream at anyone who cares to listen for the ambulance to go faster. They answer that it's already going at its maximum speed.

The ambulance jerks to a halt and abruptly discharges me at the entrance to Emergency. The woman in Intensive Care gives me an electrocardiogram and another woman digs around in my vein with the end of a needle. My sister's giving me these mild looks. I wonder what she thinks of me. I'm mad at myself for having forced her to witness this.

Pulse, blood, everything's normal. Even my weight, to my great dismay. They tell me that I can always stay for a more thorough examination, if I want. Already, my arms and legs are calmer, my heart too.

I decide to stay for the examination. My sister goes home. The longer I wait, the more idiotic I feel. Squeezed on a hospital bench with a bunch of old people watching the *The Moomins* on a giant TV screen. I remember that I had a shift at work this evening and that I'm missing it. I get more and more frustrated.

Three hours later, I see a nurse. She advises psychotherapy and eventually, antidepressants. She says that panic attacks are common in young people my age, because we live in such a crazy world. Crazy in the sense that the pace of life is accelerating; everything's speeding up.

I see myself again in the ambulance, wailing at the driver to go faster. It seems to me that I can't imagine a more accurate representation of the sorry state of humanity.

.

I receive an envelope. $270 in ambulance fees.

.

I can't take any more risks. I stop running in the street. From now on, minimal effort and minimal movement. I can't let my heart beat faster for no reason.

.

A steadily mounting state of paralysis.

First, I'm afraid to be home alone. Then, I'm afraid to leave the house alone, to walk on the street and have a cardiopulmonary arrest, a transient ischemic attack, a pulmonary embolism, a heart attack, a ruptured abdominal aneurysm, or die a sudden death from arrhythmia. I'm scared a stranger will find me lying on the ground, and it will already be too late. I don't want it to be a stranger who discovers my body, nor my parents, and especially not you. Who, when and how this will happen keeps changing in my head.

·

I practically forget that we are a couple, and this pisses you off. I don't think about you anymore. I just think of one thing, this death waiting inside me.

·

I have to have my cell phone with me, near me, on me, charged to its maximum capacity. My charger is always in my bag. I must have my Medicare card in my pocket; I should have the number tattooed on my body to be sure.

·

I resign from the perfume shop. I can no longer bear the loneliness of those whole days behind the counter, far at the back of that excessively long boutique.

·

My father gets up, with difficulty, puts his shoes on. We leave the house in pajamas. The car goes down a deserted Chambly Road, a Tuesday night. The lights dance on the wet pavement. A quarter to midnight, with its handful of prostitutes on the street corners.

My left arm hurts; I've got these dull aches in my forearm. It might be muscular. I massage it. The pain doesn't go away. One of the symptoms of a heart attack is pain in the left arm.

At Emergency, a place which is starting to feel familiar to me, the hours go by. Reassured to be within the protective walls of the hospital, I quickly fall asleep on my dad's shoulder while he reads his magazine. I hear faraway voices, the sounds of the respirator and the electrocardiogram, and then silence.

A full, intoxicating absence. I haven't felt so calm in weeks, months, maybe even years.

Time goes by in another temporality. A visit to Limbo.

·

I pass a battery of tests: blood test, electrocardiogram, scan, neurological tests. The clinics and hospitals reject my case, discredit my healthy body, my healthy but borderline weight. My thinness does not qualify for the examinations; I haven't worked on it enough. I'm in perfect health, medically speaking, normal, nothing else to say or do about it. Fuck my life very much.

·

Despite everything, I know that my body wants to betray me. I worry about the slightest pain in my stomach, or anywhere else, as if this spelled the end, as if my death knell were being sounded.

·

My periods don't return. It's a total drought. I don't feel anything, even when you are near and stuff is happening between us.

My underwear is always clean.

·

My leg hurts.

I read the booklet on the side effects of the Pill. I'm convinced that a blood clot is lodged in my vena cava. I throw away my prescription for Yasmin. Anyway, my periods disappeared so long ago; I can't imagine how my belly could conceive a child in these conditions. Moreover, we aren't doing much with our bodies that could result in any procreation.

I want to forget about death by returning to my childhood.

I shop at Costco with my parents, I follow them to the car wash, to the hardware store, to the pharmacy.

I don't pay for anything myself anymore; I play the role of the spoiled baby. They buy me a purple notebook and a pack of crayons. Obsessed by hybrid beings, I start to draw mermaids. I also write little poems about you. You don't read them, and that's a good thing. I don't write for you to read my stuff, even though you're the one I'm writing for.

I don't go out with my friends anymore. They don't call me anymore.

I'm no longer good enough for them.

Nobody knows that I go to bed with the light on and the window open so that I can hear the birds singing at dawn.

To make it through the night.

There is nothing more gentle and soothing than the sun that filters in through my curtains, and the cries of blue jays.

My eyes are sunken, dried out with fatigue.

·

I wish someone would punch me in the face so I could just crumple up and finally get some sleep.

·

I tag along with my parents on their seaside holiday in the States.

We return to my wooden carousel. The old mounts have been replaced by safe, identical horses. The lightbulbs are LED, and the speakers blast dance floor hits. Nobody's waiting in line.

The operator starts the ride and the structure shakes, gradually gains speed. My parents smile and take pictures on their cell phones. My brother and sister wait on the sidelines. The operator is visibly uncomfortable. I even suspect him of cutting the ride short.

My father comes up to me, a smile on his lips. "One more time?"

I pretend not to notice the joke.

My mother shows me the photos. The image on the little screen is of a tall girl's cadaver mounted on a plastic horse.

·

After the States, the perilous pilgrimage to the Magdalen Islands. I'm stressed out the whole trip because of the cardiac arrest I'm going to have on the highway. But the worst is the boat, where there is no operating room and probably only the most basic sort of resuscitation system on board. I pace up and down the bridge, disturbed by the vibrations of the turbines, my fingers glued to the palpitating veins of my fist.

When we arrive, I curse our island, for the simple and logical reason that it's too far from the hospital.

·

When we go to the beach, I stay close to the access roads. It seems to me that it's hard for an ambulance to drive on sand. I gather shells, stuff my pockets with them, bring them back to the house, pile them up at the foot of my bed.

One morning, my brother and I find some human bones that are clearly those of a drowned person. A piece of ribcage points in the direction of a nearby dune. A toothless jaw. We call the police. They arrive immediately and evacuate the beach.

I empty my room of all its shells. I can't collect them anymore.

·

A storm hits and lasts for days.

Under the attic, I hear my ancestors discuss my situation. Their irises shine in the darkness like fireflies. Their great-grandchild is so close. They want to welcome me into their silky dead arms.

I beg them to go away, and they do. They fly out the window and vanish in the lagoon at the bottom of the road. Their mutterings continue to obsess me even as the whole house stirs more than ever, creaking like a shipwreck.

In the morning, after I've told her about my nocturnal misadventure, my mother replies that actually, there is nothing gentler than the dead.

I don't sleep for the rest of the vacation, even though the windy nights are free of ghosts. Waiting for morning, I draw mermaids and write you emails you don't answer.

·

We walk all the way to the end of the shoal: a sandy spur digging into the Gulf. A four- hour round trip. The waves spit at my face, carrying their seal cadavers onto the shore as a warning.

In the afternoon, I refuse to climb the knolls, despite the fact I've done it a hundred times in the past. I'm already imagining a heart attack midway. I run down the hill to dive into the sea. I see my bones at the sea bottom; seaweed and periwinkles grow on them.

·

After a month at the seaside, I am welcomed back into the comforting sterility of the suburb. I feel very safe now, reconnecting with supermarkets, gigantic shopping malls, the countless drive-throughs. I reacquaint myself with the clean laundry smell of the streets, the floor-cleaner smell of the big box stores, where I shop every afternoon with my grandmother. I discover that I enjoy hanging out at the pharmacy, where I measure my blood pressure by the prescription counter. I like it when the monitor's cylinder gradually squeezes my arm; I find it reassuring.

·

I'm afraid of dying as I empty the dishwasher, I'm afraid of dying while climbing stairs, while washing my hair, while going to the bathroom. I'm afraid of dying while buying my métro pass, I'm even more afraid of dying on the métro, or while folding my clothes, or watching a movie, or shopping. I'm afraid of dying in my sleep.

It feels like my heart is going to stop from one moment to another, that the thread my life hangs from could suddenly twist around, go for my throat, and strangle me. What's more, the thread itself is taut, ready to snap at any moment. One moment of carelessness would suffice, just one moment for everything to fall, for me to fall. I therefore have to stay alert for the slightest distress signal my body sends me, in case it should decide to break down. Chest pain or discomfort. Discomfort elsewhere in the upper body. Dizzy spells. Breathlessness. Sweats. Nausea.

I dream of living in the hospital, of having a room there, just in case.

Every day is the last day of my life. I'm afraid that you won't be there, that nobody will be there to save me, or at least, to be with me as I die.

I check my pulse every five minutes, just in case it has disappeared.

You tell me: "Yes, a person can die anytime, it's true, it can happen to anyone. Everyone has to learn to deal with that, to live with that knowledge. You just tell yourself, sure, every day might be the last."

The problem is that I *can't* deal with that. My brain is stuck in emergency mode. My connections are messed up. How are you supposed to fix something like that?

I make my will. Burial or cremation?

Oh, but that's so heavy. I've been trying to make this lighter.

The day has been hot and muggy. It smells like freshly cut grass. My earphones are deep in my ears. My mother appears in the doorway. Supper's ready. I don't move. She grows impatient, shouts louder. I remain still, a magazine open on my lap. My mother comes outside, walks toward me, grumbling about those goddamn earphones that force you to scream your lungs out to be heard.

That's when she realizes that something's not right. She stops. Observes the odd angle of my neck, my head fallen to one side as if detached. Her hand grabs my shoulder, to shake it. My body slumps, revealing my face, my white eye sockets, my mouth hanging open.

My mother jumps back, screaming.

My father intervenes, shakes me the way you'd shake an apple tree, and my skull flops around in all directions. There's a bit of spittle on my cheek. My father says, "No, no, no, no," over and over again. My brother and sister get up from the table but remain dazed at the gate. My mother is lying on the ground.

A light drizzle begins to fall. My father stops trying to revive me. It's over. The pages of my *Seventeen* magazine turn in the wind, a zoetrope of svelte and smiling nymphets.

They lay my body in the short, scratchy grass, under a thin blanket of wilted dandelions. My father rolls me in the tarp from our swimming pool. He leaves just my face visible, poking out at the end, because it's the last thing you want to see disappear on someone. Everyone cries around my shroud, except for my mother, who is still unconscious.

The three of them hoist my body into the fir tree behind our house, up onto the high branches which look over the kitchen window. When my mother does the dishes that night, it will be my eyes that illuminate the room. My face will grow more and more emaciated until it completely vanishes.

.

It doesn't go away.

I no longer sleep more than one out of every two nights. After surrendering to insomnia, I slip into my parents' bed with the hope of finding sweet, soporific comfort there. Seconds later, I get up again; I don't want to die next to them. I want to save them from waking up beside my corpse.

.

The phobia of dying does not have a name yet. I'm a prisoner of this unnamed zone.

My nerves overheat and snap. I find myself throbbing with electrical shocks on the entire left side of my body. My profile stays frozen in a constant spasm, from the tips of my toes all the way up to my face. The inside of my eye is burning. There is perpetual pain radiating from the junctures of my ribs. I don't know what to do anymore, what to think. I entertain myself with failed *American Idol* auditions on YouTube, and my mother's copy of *Châtelaine*.

I don't go out anymore, except to your house, and when I do, I'm driven there, escorted.

When I go to bed, there are pearls of sweat on my back and between my breasts. I toss, turn, get up, go back to bed. You don't know what to say anymore, what to do to calm me down. You're starting to be afraid of sleeping too; you think that death is interested in you as well. I'm contaminating you, and I'm furious with myself.

Dawn has not yet risen, and the birds are already singing. A breeze sails across your room. It's going to be a beautiful day.

    I caress your back, beached next to me in bed like a boat run aground. This morning, like all mornings, your skin smells nice, like soap. I can already hear the echo of your next awakening; I imagine the alarm ringing, and your gaze at the empty pillow to your right.

I'll leave the house to walk into the river. I'll only hear the heavy current of the water on the rocks, far away, further down.

I'll be wearing this white sweater, the one I stole from you, as a shroud. And the river below will roar with pleasure as I plunge in, head first.

.

My mother receives the call around ten one quiet weeknight.

My sister is the one driving. The streets are empty. We aren't talking. The radio is hesitating between two stations, and we don't care. I haven't felt this relaxed in a long time.

We turn at the corner of our street. My sister, as usual, forgets to stop at the stop sign. I only have the time to notice the other van that is heading toward us at full speed, to our right. The time to think, Shit, that's it. And it is. The noise of scrap metal against scrap metal and of cracked glass, the absence of screams. The strength of the impact sends us spinning for an incalculable length of time.

When the car finally stops, I feel my body, my arms, I move my legs. Turn to my sister, who has turned pale blue.

"You all right?"

"I think…"

She bursts into tears. I try to reassure her with an awkward hug. I notice the completely smashed-in door on my side, the shattered window. I pick fine shards of glass from my palms. I open my door. My hands are trembling as they never have before. They leave bloody prints on the handle.

The front tire is completely destroyed, crushed under the body of the car, almost level with my seat. The shock wave goes through my body once more and culminates in a vital impulse, a powerful desire to live that will never leave me again.

·

The fear doesn't go away at all. It lingers for a long time. The palpitations, the sense of urgency, the cramps, the pacing back and forth in the middle of the night.

You can't take this anymore. No one can.

·

I have to stop lying to myself. I have to face reality.

·

One day, I go down into the métro and no longer feel that I'm in danger. I don't think about anything. I just stare at the face with the dark-ringed eyes and hollow cheeks reflected in the train window, astounded that it is actually mine.